After losing our 21 month-old son, Stewie, to an accidental drowning while on a family vacation in St. Martin in 1989, my wife Kim and I, along with our daughters Blake, Alexandra, Chase and Madison, wrote our first book, *Stewie the Duck Learns to Swim*, in the hopes of raising awareness about this preventable occurrence and saving lives.

Most drowning accidents occur in children between the ages of two and seven years-old. This is exactly the age group that this book is targeting. And for parents of boys, please be aware that they account for almost 80 percent of drownings — mostly because they are more curious and experimental.

Drowning is preventable, especially if children are taught at an early age the three simple rules that Kim and I outlined in our first book, which are repeated in the opening of this book as well — learn to swim, wear a life vest when you're near the water and always have an adult watch you when you're in the water.

Everyone kept asking us when are we going to write a second book? We'll here it is — *Swimming Lessons with Stewie the Duck*. The book is all about the skills and fears children face when they first start taking swimming lessons. We contacted swim coaches and they helped us identify the most important steps for beginning swimmers. These are to first, teach kids how to blow out of their nose. When most kids fall into the water, they panic and inhale. The next lesson is to teach them to roll onto their backs and float. Kids are great at this and it could mean the difference between life and death. Then, if they learn to kick, they can easily get to the side of the pool or shore safely.

One hundred percent of the proceeds of this book go toward the Stew Leonard III Water Safety Foundation which is committed to teaching kids to swim. I want to thank the Phoenix Children's Hospital for embracing Stewie the Duck and the National Water Safety Congress for presenting us with their first-ever national education award. We are committed to this cause and hope that reading Stewie's adventures to your children will help you avoid the tragedy that my family faced.

I'd love your feedback or, if you would like to help with our efforts please e-mail me at stewietheduck@stewleonards.com or visit www.stewietheduck.com.

Sincerely,

— Kim + Stew Leonard, Jr.

Dedicated
to our son
Stew Leonard III

Published by Kimberly Press, LLC
100 Westport Avenue, Norwalk CT 06851

Manufactured in the United States of America

ISBN: 0-9668611-3-2

First Print: May 2005

Swimming Lessons with Stewie the Duck

by Kim and Stew Leonard

Illustrated by
Vicky Lowe

designed by
Rich Lung

Stewie's mom opened the curtains to her
son's bedroom, letting the sun shine in.
"Good morning, Stewie," she said.
"What are you singing on this beautiful morning?"
"The water safety song, Mom!" Stewie said.
"Swimming is so much fun!"

4

Later that morning at breakfast, Stewie asked,
"Mom, how do I learn to swim without my life vest?"
"Well, Stewie, you have to take more swimming lessons,"
Mom replied.
"Would you like to do that, Stewie?
Take more swimming lessons?" his Dad asked.
"You bet!" said Stewie.

At Stewie's first swimming lesson, he met his coach, Rob.
There were four other students in Stewie's swimming class —
Hunter the Puppy, Cameron the Frog, Susannah the Swan,
and Avery the Otter.
"Good morning, kids!" Coach Rob said, blowing on his whistle.
"Is everyone excited about learning to swim?"
"Yeah, yeah, yeah!" the kids yelled.

"Good!" Coach Rob said. "Before we start, you have to learn a few things about being around a pool. Most important of all is that
YOU MUST ALWAYS LISTEN TO ME
AND FOLLOW MY INSTRUCTIONS.
"Yes, Coach Rob!" said the swim class students.
"O.K., now can anybody tell me what this
big round thing is?" he asked.
"It looks like a giant candy!" said Susannah.
"It's called a ring buoy," Rob explained.
"If someone is drowning or is in trouble in the water,
you throw this to them. It helps them float."

7

"There's another thing you need to know before you learn to swim,"
Coach Rob went on. "That's how to get into the water safely.
We don't jump, and we never push anyone else in.
We just hold onto the side of the pool and carefully
slide into the water."

Stewie carefully slid into the water. So did the others.

"The first thing we're going to do is learn how to put our faces in the water and blow bubbles," Coach Rob said.
"This is the easy part!" Stewie whispered to Avery.
"Watch me!" And he stuck his face in the water.
Stewie loved blowing bubbles.

Avery watched Stewie blow bubbles
but wouldn't put her face in the water.
"Blowing bubbles is baby stuff!" she said holding
onto the side of the pool. "What do we learn next?"
Coach Rob noticed that Avery wasn't blowing bubbles,
but decided to wait and see what happened
before he said anything. "Look at all the bubbles!" he said.
"Let's all sing a song about bubbles."

Sing along to: Row, Row, Row Your Boat!"

Blow, blow,
blow real hard
Bubbles fill the pool
That's how it goes,
just blow through your nose
It's fun at swimming
school!

11

"Next we are going to learn how to kick while holding onto the edge of the pool," Coach Rob said.
"I can do that!" Hunter said.
"It's just like kicking a ball at school!"
"This is fun!" said Stewie happily.
"Look at me, Dad!"
"Let's all sing this song about kicking!" Coach Rob suggested.

12

Kick, kick, kick real hard
Kick just like a mule!
I can splash and get all wet
It's fun at swimming school!

Sing along to: Row, Row, Row Your Boat!"

13

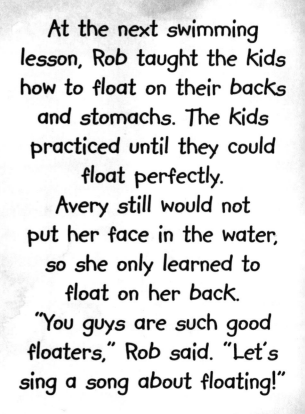

At the next swimming lesson, Rob taught the kids how to float on their backs and stomachs. The kids practiced until they could float perfectly.

Avery still would not put her face in the water, so she only learned to float on her back.

"You guys are such good floaters," Rob said. "Let's sing a song about floating!"

14

Sing along to: Row, Row, Row Your Boat!"

Float, float, float all day
I'm feeling pretty cool
I can float on my
stomach or back
It's fun at swimming school!

15

Then Coach Rob taught them
to roll over on their backs
whenever they were too tired to
swim anymore. "This is a good
trick to use whenever you feel
pooped," Rob explained.
"Once you're on your back,
you can kick your way to
the side of the pool.
And you can always call
for help if you need to.
Let's all sing about rolling
on your back."

16

Sing along to: Row, Row, Row Your Boat!"

Roll, roll on your back
The most important rule.
If you're tired,
just use this trick
It's fun at
swimming school

17

After the kids were out of the water,
Coach Rob had something to tell them.
"At your next swimming lesson,
I'm going to test you on
blowing bubbles, floating and kicking." he said.
"If you pass, you'll get a special graduation medal."

Stewie couldn't wait to take the swimming test.
"I'm going to get a medal!" he told everyone at dinner.
"Congratulations, Stewie!" said his sister Blake.
"We know you can do it," added his next-door neighbor, Alexandra.
"You're going to be a great swimmer!" said his other sister, Chase.
Baby Madison clapped her wings.
"Yeah, Stewie!" she quacked.

The day of the swimming test, Stewie was getting ready
to go into the pool when he heard someone crying.
It was Avery.
"What's wrong?" Stewie asked.
"I'm going to fail the swimming test!" Avery sniffed.
"I...I...I can't put my face in the water!
I can't blow bubbles! I can't!"

"How come?" Stewie asked.
"When I was little, I got water up my nose once,
and it hurt," Avery said sadly.
"That happened to me, too," Stewie said.
"But my big sister Blake taught me a trick.
If you just keep blowing
bubbles out of your nose,
you won't have that problem."
"Hmm," Avery said.
"Maybe I'll try it...."

Coach Rob stood at the edge
of the pool with his clipboard.
The test was about to begin.
"I'm scared!" whispered Avery. "I can't do it!"
"Yes you can," Stewie said.
"I'll stay right next to you.
You're going to be a great
swimmer—I just know it."
"Okay," Coach Rob said.
"You first, Stewie! Let me see
you blow some bubbles!"

23

Stewie popped his face in the water and blew a stream of *bubbles* out of his nose. "Very good, Stewie," Coach Rob said, making a check on his clipboard. "Now let's see what else you can do!"

Stewie flipped
on his back
and kicked.

He floated on his back
for thirty seconds.

And he paddled
safely to the edge
of the pool.

25

"Very good, Stewie!" said Coach Rob, making check marks on his clipboard. "Now it's your turn, Avery!"

Avery looked at Stewie. She looked down at the water.
Then she took a deep breath, put her face in the water,
and blew the biggest bubbles Stewie had ever seen.
She had done it! "Good work, Avery," said Coach Rob smiling.
"Those were really big bubbles!"

26

Then Avery flipped on
her back and kicked.

Next, she floated on her
back for thirty seconds.

Finally, she paddled safely
over to the edge of the
pool, where Stewie
was waiting.

27

Coach Rob put four checks next to Avery's name.
"Very good, Avery. You passed!
You're going to get your swimming medal!"
"I knew you could do it!" Stewie said.
"I couldn't have done it without you, Stewie," Avery said.
"You're the best swimming buddy ever!"
Coach Rob then gave Stewie the Duck, Cameron the Frog,
Avery the Otter, Susannah the Swan and
Hunter the Puppy their swimming medals.
"Congratulations, everyone!
Let's all sing the swimming song one more time!"

Blow, blow, blow real hard
Bubbles fill the pool
That's how it goes, just blow through your nose
It's fun at swimming school!

Kick, kick, kick real hard
Kick just like a mule
I can splash and get all wet
It's fun at swimming school!

Float, float, float all day
I'm feeling pretty cool
I can float on my stomach or back
It's fun at swimming school!

Roll, roll on your back
The most important rule.
If you're tired, just use this trick
It's fun at swimming school!

Some Water Safety
TIPS for Parents

ABC's of Water Safety(TM)

Water Watchers at Phoenix Children's Hospital recommends that
every family develop a water safety plan, by practicing the
ABC's of Water Safety:

A is for Adult:

Adults need to have eye-to-eye contact with children around all forms
of water. (pools, bathtubs, buckets, canals, etc.)

B is for Barrier:

Supervision is critical, but can fail. To prevent a drowning, multiple
barriers should be placed between kids and water. Barriers can include
fences, alarms, door and window locks that are out of children's reach,
and self-closing, self-latching hardware on doors. Barriers around other
forms of water include lids on buckets, locks on bathroom doors,
and toilet locks.

C is for Classes:

For adults, this means CPR classes taken regularly to keep your skills
fresh, for children at the appropriate age, this means swimming and
water safety classes.

THANK YOU
to the following sponsors
for helping make this publication possible.

Ferguson Family

Barbara & Gary Johnson & Family

Kendall-Jackson Winery

Bank of America

Coca-Cola Company

Cargill Value Added Meats

Kleiman & Hochberg

Newman's Own

Price Waterhouse Coopers

Poland Springs

Quality Sales

All proceeds from book sales go towards the
Stew Leonard III Water Safety Foundation. Each year,
the Foundation provides scholarships for swim lessons and also
donates water safety equipment to local YMCAs.
In addition, the Foundation sponsors water safety awareness events,
including book readings, children's concerts and health fairs.
For more information, visit www.stewietheduck.com.

It's Fun at Swimming School

(Sung to the tune of Row, Row Row Your Boat)

1. Blow, blow, blow real hard — bub-bles fill the pool
2. Float, float, float all day, I'm feel-ing pret-ty cool

That's how it goes — just blow through your nose, It's fun at swim-ming school
I—can float on my stom-ach or back, It's fun at swim-ming school!

Kick, kick, kick real hard — Kick just like a mule
Roll, roll on your back, The most im-por-tant rule

I can splash—and get all wet, It's fun at swim-ming school!
If you're tired, just use this trick, It's fun at swim-ming school!